Big Train

Big Train

Richard Brignall

James Lorimer & Company, Ltd., Publishers
Toronto

James Lorimer & Company Ltd. acknowledges the support of the Canada Council for the Arts and the Ontario Arts Council for our publishing program. We acknowledge the financial support of the Government of Canada through the Book Publishing Industry Development Program (BPIDP) for our publishing activities. We acknowledge the Government of Ontario through the Ontario Media Development Corporation's Ontario Book Initiative.

Library and Archives Canada Cataloguing in Publication

Brignall, Richard
    Big Train : the legendary ironman of sport, Lionel Conacher / Richard Brignall.

(Recordbooks)
ISBN 978-1-55277-451-9 (bound).—ISBN 978-1-55277-450-2 (pbk.)

    1. Conacher, Lionel, 1900-1954—Juvenile literature.
2. Athletes—Canada—Biography—Juvenile literature.
3. Canada. Parliament. House of Commons—Biography—Juvenile literature. 4. Legislators—Canada—Biography—Juvenile literature.
5. Ontario. Legislative Assembly—Biography—Juvenile literature.
6. Legislators—Ontario—Biography—Juvenile literature.

I. Title. II. Series: Record books

GV697.C63B75 2009   j796'.092   C2009-901681-8

James Lorimer & Company Ltd., Publishers
317 Adelaide Street West,
Suite #1002
Toronto, ON
M5V 1P9
www.lorimer.ca

Distributed in the U.S. by:
Orca Book Publishers
P.O. Box 468
Custer, WA USA
98240-0468

Printed and bound in Canada.

Contents

I would like to dedicate this book to all the newspaper, magazine, and book editors who have given me a chance to write for them over the years. They have guided me to where I am today. Without them I would not be living out my dream and writing books like this one.

Thank You.

Prologue

It looked like the Yale baseball squad would lose again. It was the bottom of the ninth inning and they were down by one run. The Harvard pitcher only needed three more outs to win the game.

Yale's first batter flied out to the centre fielder. The second batter grounded to the shortstop and was thrown out at first. The game was over in most people's eyes. The fans who filled the stands were getting ready to leave after the final out. Even the

Yale batboy gathered up the bats not thinking Yale would start a rally.

But Yale wasn't ready to give up. The third batter hit the ball over the third baseman's glove for a single.

Frank Merriwell stepped up to bat with the game-tying run on first base. He hadn't got a hit all day. The Harvard pitcher thought he would be another easy out. A Harvard victory was certain.

Merriwell swung wildly and missed the first two pitches. One more miss and the game was over. He then watched two more pitches fly past him. Merriwell had a good eye as they were both balls.

The Harvard pitcher then delivered the hardest pitch he could throw. It looked like it could be strike three. Frank gripped the bat tight and swung as hard as he could. A loud crack echoed through the ballpark as Merriwell's bat connected with the ball. The ball flew over the second baseman's head into right field.

Everybody yelled for Merriwell to run. He ran to first while the right fielder ran for the ball. Frank kept on running for second. After he touched second base the other base runner made it home to tie the score.

There was so much noise Frank could not hear the coaches, but he saw that the fielder still did not have the ball. He made third, and the excited coach sent him home.

Every man, woman, and child was standing. It seemed as if everyone was shouting and waving flags, hats, or handkerchiefs. If Merriwell reached home, Yale would win. If he failed, the score would be tied.

The fielder had the ball. He threw it to the shortstop who whirled around and sent it whistling home. The catcher was ready to stop Merriwell.

Frank slid into home plate. At the same time the catcher got the ball and tried to tag Frank out. It was hard to see through the cloud of dust whether he'd made it or not.

A sudden silence filled the ballpark as they waited for the umpire's decision.

"Safe home!" rang the voice of the umpire.

The crowd roared with excitement. Not even the school band could be heard over the cheering.

The Yale players surrounded Frank and cheered him on. They then grabbed him and put him on their shoulders. They carried him off the field as the crowd continued to cheer.

★★★

Frank Merriwell could do anything to save the day. He could score a tie-breaking goal, steal home for the winning run, or run for the winning touchdown. He was always the hero. But that was easy for somebody who wasn't real. Merriwell was a fictional character in children's books written in the early 1900s.

Even though Merriwell was not real, he inspired young readers. Those readers dreamed of being sports heroes. Each one wanted to be the player who always won the game with a great last-minute play. One of these dreamers was young Lionel Conacher in Toronto's North End.

"I wanted above all else to emulate the great Frank Merriwell of fiction and longed in every bit of me to … rise upon demand to great heights," said Lionel.

1 Hard Work Pays Off

Frank Merriwell was the star in a series of sports stories for children. In these stories, Merriwell excelled at many sports at Yale University while solving mysteries and righting wrongs. The stories appeared in a magazine starting on April 18, 1896. One story was published each week until 1912. Merriwell's adventures also appeared in 209 short books, called dime novels, between 1896 and 1930. Author Gilbert Patten, under the pen name Burt L.

Standish, created Merriwell and wrote most of the stories.

Lionel Conacher did not live a fictional life like Merriwell. Lionel faced great hardship while growing up in one of the poorest neighbourhoods in Toronto.

But Lionel would go on to become a great athlete, a real–life Frank Merriwell. Lionel played many different sports and was always the star. Each season had its own sport, and Lionel never seemed to take a season off. It was football in the fall, hockey in the winter, and baseball and lacrosse in the summer. Lionel played all these sports as an amateur and a professional.

Today, pro athletes play one sport. They are focused on being the best in that sport. An athlete might try to play two different pro sports, but it never works out. Today, sports seasons are long, and they overlap. Athletes must decide which sport they want to play.

But there was a time when athletes could play different sports through the year. This was when Lionel Conacher became one of Canada's greatest all-round athletes.

Even great athletes have simple beginnings. Childhood is when a person is affected by many different influences on a path to greatness. There would be many influences in Lionel's life. None would be greater than his family.

On May 24, 1900, in Toronto, Ontario, Lionel Pretoria Conacher was born. Lionel was the name of an ancestor and Pretoria was a well-known South African city during the Boer War. Lionel Conacher was the oldest boy and third of ten children born to Benjamin and Elizabeth Conacher.

Ben Conacher drove his horse and wagon to many jobs to make a living. A typical workday in the winter started at five in the morning. He would travel two hours to work on Toronto's Centre Island. He would cut squares of ice out of the lake all day. They were stored to keep food cold in the summer.

Ben earned $7.50 each week. That was not enough to support his family. During the winter he hitched a plough to his horse and cleaned snow off the ice rinks at Jesse Ketchum Park. The extra dollar he received each night helped make ends meet.

Almost everything came the hard way for the Conachers. The parents worked hard to put food on the table. They worked to make their home rich in love and moral support. Elizabeth Conacher also set the rules of behaviour in the home.

By 1912, Ben was being paid nine dollars per week. One night, twelve-year-old Lionel was busy helping his father. Ben had been asked by his boss to hire another man to help haul sod from Don Valley. Lionel begged his father to let him do the job. He said over and over, "I can do it, I can do it." His father eventually agreed.

The next morning at five, Lionel did not get up and get ready for school. Instead he drove a team of horses to the Don Valley. He loaded the wagon with sod and then delivered it around the city. He did this for ten hours. The long day of work proved Lionel could do it. More importantly, he earned an extra dollar for the family.

This job taught Lionel at a young age that hard work and determination are keys to success. He learned that if he worked hard enough, he could do almost anything.

2 Discovering Sport

The other influence in Lionel's early life was where he lived. His Toronto neighbourhood was a working-class area where money was tight.

The Conacher house was on Davenport Road, three doors down from Jesse Ketchum Park and School. The park had a large open field and two ice rinks. When Lionel was old enough, he went to the school.

In a poor neighbourhood like Ketchum,

playing sports helped kids forget about where they lived and how tough times were. One thing they always had was sport.

But sport was never important to Lionel's parents. No relative on either side of the family ever played sports. Ben and Elizabeth didn't expect their children to become interested in sports. That was, until Lionel's older sister Dorothy became the family's first sports star. She earned a name around Toronto as a great runner.

Lionel first got into sport as a young child. Dressed in old clothes, he wandered over to the park where a pickup game of football was being played. He knew nothing of the rules. He was much less skilled than the other children. But he caught the sports bug. He wanted to play more.

At Jesse Ketchum School, Lionel felt the influence of principal William Kirk. Kirk believed sport was important in a child's growth. He wanted every student to take part in some organized sport.

With this in mind, Lionel started exploring other sports. He played football in the fall. He played on baseball and lacrosse teams in the spring and summer.

In the winter, Lionel wanted to play hockey. But hockey was too expensive. He couldn't afford the skates and equipment.

So he played less-expensive sports. By the time he was 14 years old, Lionel had impressed everyone with his ability in football, baseball, and lacrosse. He was always determined to win. Many people wanted Lionel to join their teams and sporting organizations.

By 1916, Lionel's list of sports included boxing and wrestling. That year he won the 61-kg (135-pound) wrestling championship of Ontario. Four years later, in 1920, he won the light-heavyweight amateur boxing championship of Canada.

Boys playing lacrosse in a field at Jesse Ketchum Park.

Whatever Lionel put his mind to, he eventually excelled at. When he was 16, he still wanted to join a hockey team. He could finally afford to get the skates and equipment he needed to play.

Lionel spent long hours learning to play

hockey.

"The average kid starts skating at the age of seven years or younger," said Lionel. "I laced on skates for the first time at the age of sixteen and you'll never know the humiliation and utter dreariness of the long hours which I spent on the rinks with younger and much more skilled players before I won a post in junior circles."

He won a position on the Toronto Century Rovers junior team. A year later he joined the Aura Lee junior club, a neighbourhood team.

When Lionel started with Aura Lee, he was given very little playing time. He rode the bench. He needed to improve his skills. He used that 1917–18 season to teach himself hockey.

Lionel had to learn how to play better hockey. He thought the best way was to watch the star players. He knew if he played like them he would get more ice time.

All his watching from the bench paid off. The next season, he became a starting defenceman. Defence is not a flashy position, but Lionel could make it exciting. He would take the puck and rush down the ice. He scored many goals this way. He also defended well, playing entire games without a rest.

The Aura Lee club started the 1918–19 season on a winning streak. Game highlights were featured in the newspaper. Lionel was seen as one of the stars of the team. The other star was forward Billy Burch. These two players formed a lifelong friendship.

Lionel must have impressed the right people in the playoffs. He was picked to join the Toronto Canoe Club, seen as Toronto's all-star junior OHA team. The team played with just one line and two

Organizing Sport

Athletic clubs were popular from the 1870s up until the 1950s. They sponsored teams to play in various sports leagues. Rowing and canoeing were the first sports to be organized in Canada by these clubs. All other sports teams kept the club's original name. That is how a Canoe Club could win a hockey or football championship.

substitutes. So these were eight of the best young hockey players in Toronto.

Lionel was joined by Aura Lee teammate Billy Burch. Other notable picks were goaltender Roy Worters and Duke McCurry, two more teammates who would become close friends to Lionel.

The Toronto Canoe Club only lost two games during the 1919–20 regular season. At the time they were considered the best junior team to ever represent Toronto. The Canoe Club swept through the OHA and

Eastern Canadian playoffs.

The newspapers praised the play of Lionel during these matches.

"Conacher was great both defensively and offensively, as he has been all season," wrote the *Toronto Star*. "He held his head under a lot of abuse. He took butt-ends and charges with a smile."

The Canoe Club went on to the national junior championship. It was a two-game series, and the team with the most total goals won. In the final, they defeated the Selkirk Fisherman by scores of 9–1 and 5–4. The Canoe Club was awarded the Memorial Cup.

By this time Lionel had been successful in just about every sport he'd tried. The list included football, hockey, baseball, lacrosse, boxing, and wrestling. As a teenager he played on 14 different teams and won 11 championships.

Lionel was just at the start of an athletic

career unequaled in the history of Canadian sport.

Memorial Cup

The Memorial Cup was donated as a memorial to the Canadians who died during World War I. It became the trophy given to the junior hockey team that wins the Canadian championship. It was first awarded in 1919.

3 Emerging Star

By 1920, Lionel Conacher was in demand. He had mastered every sport he played. He was the best all-round athlete in Toronto. Clubs and teams across the city desperately wanted him to play for them. Even pro clubs wanted Lionel. Hockey was the primary pro sport in Canada. The Toronto St. Pats of the National Hockey League (NHL) offered Lionel $3,000 to play the 1920–21 season. That amount was three times the average NHL salary at the time.

Lionel turned down the offer. He knew he was not ready to make the jump to pro hockey. Going pro would take away his amateur status. He didn't want to lose the freedom to play other sports at the amateur level.

Football was the main reason Lionel wanted to keep his amateur status. It was his favourite sport. But there was no pro football league in Canada. So, once he went pro, he might never play football again.

It might seem weird that football was Lionel's favourite game. In hockey he'd just won a national championship and been offered a pro contract. He'd worked hard to reach that level. But hockey didn't come easy to him, while football did.

And football thrilled him like no other sport could. It was the first sport he'd played as a child. It became the first sport he played on a team in an organized

Lionel suited up for a football game. Not much protected players from opposition tacklers in those days.

league. Actually, for a while, it was the only organized sport he could afford to play. This was because all his equipment was provided.

Origins of Canadian Football

Rugby football started in the United Kingdom. British soldiers introduced it to Canada during the 1860s, and it became known in the U.S. after that. Over time, both Canada and the U.S. changed the rules of the game to create their own versions of rugby football. By the 1900s, the North American game was very different from the rugby football introduced in the 1860s, and came to be known as just football. Even today, some of the rules of football in Canada and the U.S. are different.

As a 12-year-old in 1912, Lionel had joined the Capitals football team. They played in the 43-kg (95-pound) division of the Toronto Rugby Football League. Lionel played a position called the middle wing. His job was to tackle the opposition when they ran with the ball. But it was the player who ran with the ball and scored touchdowns, not the tackler, who got all the attention.

Lionel played middle wing for the Capital's team, in different weight divisions, from 1912 to 1915. His team won the city championship each of these seasons.

By 1918 Lionel had moved up to the junior ranks. He played middle wing with the Toronto Central YMCA club in the Ontario Rugby Football Union (ORFU). The team won the Ontario Championship. But Lionel did not show any signs of developing into a star player.

Lionel's standing as a football player would change in 1919. He joined the Capital intermediate team in the ORFU, but not in his usual middle wing position.

As Lionel got older his body grew and he gained weight. His new coach, Mike Rodden, saw this growth and wanted to try something new. He moved Lionel from middle wing to ball carrier.

Lionel was now part of the offence. It was his job to run the ball up the field to score touchdowns. But this was only a test. If Lionel couldn't score, Rodden's experiment would end. Lionel would be moved back to his old, boring middle–wing position.

The change could have been hard for Lionel. In those days, there was no such thing as blocking for ball carriers. He had to rely totally upon his own skill to evade opposing players when running down the field.

But Rodden was right. Lionel's size and speed made him perfect for running the ball. He thrived in his new position. He proved unstoppable when he ran with the ball. He became the star of the league.

Lionel led the Capitals of Toronto to the ORFU final. They faced a Sarnia squad for the championship. Sarnia put all their effort into stopping Lionel. Sarnia's plan worked, and they won the championship.

Even though Lionel's team had lost, the game showed how great a player he had become that year. Stopping him was the difference between a team winning or losing. Lionel was ready to join the highest level of football in Canada.

At that time there was no Canadian Football League (CFL). There was no single national league. The champions of the various senior leagues across Canada played off for the national championship. The winners were awarded the Grey Cup.

In eastern Canada there were three senior football leagues. The Inter-provincial Union included familiar teams such as the Toronto Argonauts and the Ottawa Rough Riders. The Inter-collegiate Union included teams from the

The Grey Cup

In 1909, Lord Earl Grey, the Governor General of Canada, donated a trophy to be awarded to the amateur rugby football champions of Canada. It became known as the Grey Cup. The first championship game was played in 1901 between the University of Toronto and the Parkdale Canoe Club. The University of Toronto won. The trophy is still played for each year by the top teams in the CFL.

University of Toronto and Queen's University. The third senior league was the Ontario Rugby Football Union (ORFU). In the ORFU, both the Parkdale Canoe Club and the Toronto Rugby Club wanted to sign Lionel. He eventually joined the Toronto Rugby Club, also known as the Torontos.

Everyone expected a lot of Lionel. He was seen as the league's emerging.

The Torontos played the opening match against Parkdale. The Parkdale team was likely still bitter about losing Lionel to the Torontos. Lionel's play made the taste in their mouths even more sour. He opened the scoring with a touchdown. Later in the game he made a 50-yard dash down the field. Parkdale stopped him on their goal line. On the next play Lionel was handed the ball. He easily scored his second touchdown of the game. The Torontos won 28–12.

It would be another successful football season for Lionel in 1920. The Toronto Rugby club won the ORFU senior championship, and Lionel was a large part of that win. He was a marvel when he rushed the ball for a touchdown. That season he also worked as a kicker. He scored many points that way.

The Torontos faced the Toronto Argonauts in the 1920 Grey Cup semi-final playoff. The Argos were the favourites going into the game. They were champions of the Inter-provincial league, which was seen as the best in Canada.

At the halfway mark, the Argos had only a 2–0 lead. By the end of the third quarter, Lionel's team was winning 6–2.

"The game served to show that all the good things claimed of Lionel Conacher are no exaggeration," wrote the *Star*. "Conacher held his own in kicking and once under way, proved the hardest man on the field to stop."

The fans got excited when Lionel ran the ball. He ran his way through the opposing team. With his great strength he left a trail of wounded players behind him.

Lionel was playing a great game against the Argos. But it was not a game one man could win alone. The Argos were more experienced and didn't rely on a single player to win.

In the fourth quarter, the Argos scored five points. By the final bell, that was enough for a 7–6 victory. The Argos headed to the Grey Cup final. They would lose that game to the University of Toronto Varsity.

4 Iron Man

It was a hot summer afternoon when Lionel Conacher went from being a local sports star to a sports legend in Toronto. On June 21, 1921, he performed what people called the "Iron Man stunt." It was an unbelievable feat that surprised even his teammates. But Lionel simply didn't want to miss a game.

At 21 years of age, Lionel was considered Toronto's greatest all-round athlete. He performed at a high level in every sport he played. He usually switched the sports he played by the season. On that one summer day he switched sports by the hour.

Lionel started the day with the Hillcrest baseball club. Going into the final inning, Hillcrest was down by a single run. They started a comeback and loaded the bases. It was up to Lionel to hit them all home.

With victory on the line, Lionel cracked a double to centre field. The bases cleared and Hillcrest won the game.

As the Hillcrest players enjoyed their victory, Lionel was nowhere in sight. After getting the game-winning hit, he had run from the field to a waiting car.

As the car drove across the city, Lionel changed his baseball uniform for his lacrosse outfit. He joined his lacrosse team, the Maitlands, at halftime. The Maitlands were losing 2–1 to a Brampton team.

The addition of Lionel boosted his

team's attack in the third quarter. The Maitlands tied the score less than three minutes after he appeared on the field.

The Maitlands took the lead early in the fourth quarter with another goal. Then Lionel rushed in alone on the Brampton goal and put himself on the score sheet. His team was ahead 4–2.

Two goals down, Brampton sent all players down on the attack. It was a desperate final effort to win the game. In the scramble, Lionel got the ball. He raced out of the mass of players and headed for the Brampton goal. Most of the Brampton team chased him down the field.

Lionel had the speed and endurance to avoid being caught. He bored down on the Brampton net. Only the netminder was between him and another goal. The goalie took the only chance he had. He charged out of the net toward Lionel. They collided hard.

When the dust cleared, the goalie was doing a flip in the air. The ball was in the net. Thanks to Lionel, the Maitlands won the match 5–3.

5 Breaking Through the Line

By the time he'd turned 19, Lionel realized he wasn't a child anymore. He knew he needed to do something to help pay the bills at home. But he worried that it might be hard for him to get a good job. He'd never finished school and he didn't have a trade. The only thing he knew was sports. He quickly figured sports would be the way he could make a living.

He once told his brother Charlie, "If you want to live better you've got to make good at something and I don't know where we're going to do it if it isn't in sports."

Lionel needed a way to make money. But he didn't want to become a pro. He still wanted to play various sports as an amateur.

Lionel was lucky enough to attract many wealthy fans. This was how he could make money and still play amateur sports.

Toronto Star reporter Lou Marsh noted that Lionel was very popular among the rich and powerful fans of sports in Toronto. Harry Ardiel was one of these men. Along with being an avid sportsman, he was a banker with the Toronto–Dominion Bank. He became Lionel's friend and gave him a banking job that would pay him well. Ardiel wanted Lionel to be able to continue to play sports as an amateur.

There was one small hitch to the job. He was hired so he could play on the teams sponsored by the T-D Bank. Ardiel also hired Lionel's friend Billy Burch. Both would play for the T-D hockey team in the Toronto Bankers League. Conacher and Burch helped the team win the city and national banker titles during the 1919–20 season.

Ardiel was also involved with other teams in other sports. Lionel played for all of them. This included the Hillcrest Athletic Club baseball team and the Maitlands lacrosse organization.

The most important club Ardiel was involved in was the Toronto Argonauts football club. Lionel had impressed the team in the 1920 Grey Cup playoff. It wasn't hard for Ardiel to talk Lionel into joining. Lionel had always wanted to play on one of the Inter-provincial Union teams known as the Big Four.

Lionel's move was announced before the start of the 1921 season. The club and its supporters, including Ardiel, thought he might be what the Argos needed to win the Grey Cup.

At 21, Lionel was 180 cm (6 feet, 1 inch) tall and weighed 84 kg (185 pounds). For a big man he was fast. When he ran down the field he pumped his knees waist-high. It was almost like he was galloping. He was more likely to run over opponents than around them. He could rip a hole through opposing lines at will.

Lionel would have help producing touchdowns for the Argos. He played alongside Harry "Red" Bastone. They worked well together. Bastone would draw the opponents toward him, then pass the ball to the side to Lionel. Lionel would burst into the open and run down the field for a touchdown.

Players like Lionel and Red were important to teams that wanted to win. At this point in football history, the forward pass was not allowed. Instead of a quarterback passing the ball up the field to a receiver, these players would produce offence by running with the ball in a group. When the ball carrier got into trouble, he would lateral pass (to the side) to a teammate. Offensive players would double- or triple-pass the ball as they drove down the field. This made for exciting plays.

Lionel lived up to his hype as a great player. In his first game as an Argo, he scored 23 of the team's 27 points.

In a game against the Ottawa Rough Riders, Lionel proved unstoppable. The Argonauts won 28–5 with Lionel scoring 21 of the points.

"Conacher, of course, is the dominant figure and it was noticeable on Saturday that when he was on the sidelines the Argos' attack lost its punch," wrote the *Star.* "But, when he came back on the field

Argonaut Origins

The Argonaut Rowing Club was formed in Toronto, Ontario, in 1872. The name was taken from the mythical Greek ship the Argo, and the heroes who sailed her, the Argonauts. Members formed the Toronto Argonauts football team in 1873 as an off-season training activity. It is one of the oldest football clubs in North America. The club has won 15 Grey Cups. Nicknames for the team include the Argos, Boatmen, Oarsmen, and Double Blue (after the dark and light blue colours taken from the rowing teams of English universities Oxford and Cambridge).

in the final period he scored a couple of touchdowns in very easy fashion."

The Argonauts finished the regular season with a perfect record of six wins and no losses. They were the Big Four champions. Lionel led the league in scoring with 85 points.

The team's great play continued into the playoff match against Inter-collegiate champion University of Toronto Varsity. The Argos beat the Varsity team 20–12.

Before the 1921 season, no team from Western Canada had ever come east to challenge for the Grey Cup. The Edmonton Eskimos made history in 1921. After winning the Western Canadian championship, they travelled across Canada to Toronto. They wanted to win the Grey Cup.

The Eskimos were in the stands during the Eastern final between the Argos and Parkdale. Whoever won would play Edmonton for the Grey Cup.

It should have been an easy win for the Argos against the ORFU champions. But nothing came easy for the Argos that day.

At halftime the game was tied at 7. The Argonauts used the second half to pull out a 16–8 victory. If not for Lionel, their season would have ended with that game.

"Conacher must be given the share of credit, for without his brilliant performance it is very doubtful if the Argos would have won," wrote the *Star*. "Except for Conacher, the Oarsmen were in no way superior to the team they conquered."

It would be an Edmonton Eskimos vs. Toronto Argonauts Grey Cup match. After the game the Argos had played against Parkdale, the westerners had little fear of them as a team. The only thing they feared was Lionel and his ability to run the ball.

"The teams would have been evenly matched had Conacher not been playing with the Argos," said Eskimos coach Deacon White after the Argos–Parkdale game. "He has legs on him like an ox. If he can't get past a man he charges over him."

Almost 10,000 people packed into Varsity Stadium at the University of

Toronto for the Grey Cup game. It was the first real Canadian championship game ever played. People didn't know what to expect. They had never seen a Western Canadian football team play before. Before that year, whoever won the Eastern championship was instantly awarded the Grey Cup.

Before the championship game, the Eskimos boasted that their line of tacklers had not been crossed all year. But they had never played against a player like Lionel. The Argonauts were seen as the favourites to win.

Once the game started, the Argos quickly dashed the hopes of the Eskimos. The Argos easily smashed through their line of tackle. It took the Argos less than five minutes to score their first touchdown. Twice after that Lionel raced across the Eskimo line to score.

In the first three quarters, Lionel scored

15 points on two touchdowns, a field goal, and two single kicked points. He probably would have scored more if he had stayed in the game. Instead of playing the final quarter he left the field. He jumped into a waiting car and went across the city to play a hockey game. He knew his football team would win. He didn't want to miss his hockey team's opening game of the season.

The Argos won the Grey Cup, defeating the Eskimos 23–0. Some say Lionel won the Grey Cup for the Argos. His efforts in the game made the papers right across Canada.

A Western First

The first Western Canadian team to win the Grey Cup was the Winnipeg Football Club, in 1935. They would later change their name to the Blue Bombers.

6 The Big Train Vs.

Sportswriters were looking for the perfect way to describe Lionel. Over the years, they thought up a large list of nicknames for him. They called him Connie, Lion, the Blond Express, Iron Man, Athletic Superman, the Human Dynamo, Big Moose, and Wonder Man of Canadian Athletics. But the most popular nickname for Lionel Conacher came from his skills at football. When he raced down the field, they said he was like a powerful steam

Other Big Trains

Dr. Smirle Lawson was the original Big Train in Canada. The hard-charging football player led the University of Toronto Varsity to a Grey Cup championship in 1909. He also guided the Toronto Argonauts to two straight Grey Cup finals. Another Big Train in sport was Walter Johnson, a major-league baseball pitcher in the U.S. He was called the Big Train because of the speed of his fastball.

engine. At the same time, sports fans enjoyed comparing players from different time periods. Football fans had a young star in Lionel. With his grand rushes down the field they instantly compared him to former player Smirle Lawson.

The comparison was spot on. Lionel played the game like Lawson. Both players were unstoppable when they ran through the opposition. This is why Lawson was

It always took more than one player to bring down the original Big Train, Smirle Lawson.

given the nickname the Big Train.

After Lionel's Grey Cup performance the torch passed from Smirle Lawson to Lionel. They now called Lionel the Big

Train. It was the name he would go by for the rest of his life.

Lionel's popularity soared to new heights in 1922. People wanted to not only watch him play sports, but also meet him in person. Lionel gave his fans many chances to do both.

One public appearance Lionel made was at Christie Street Hospital. He came to the hospital on October 11, 1922, to fight Jack Dempsey.

Jack Dempsey was a famous American boxer who held the World Heavyweight title from 1919 to 1926. He had no idea he was going to step into the boxing ring that day in 1922.

When Dempsey arrived at the hospital he thought he would just smile and shake people's hands. But everybody who could stand up, walk, limp, crutch it, or be wheeled around waited in the hospital gym. The gathering surprised Dempsey.

"You don't expect me to make a speech to these boys," Dempsey said.

"Oh, no," replied Col McMean, the event organizer. "The boys want to see you box."

"Sure," Dempsey almost yelled, because he was nervous about saying a speech. "I'll box. I haven't any gloves, trunks, or shoes, but dig me up something. I'd go on barefoot, sooner than talk. Who'll I box?"

Lionel was there, ready to take on the champion.

The fight was an exhibition, and no hard punches were to be thrown. But somebody offered Lionel $100 to hit Dempsey with a good one. When the opening bell rang, Lionel went over to Dempsey and punched him hard on the chin. That sent the champion back on his heels with a bump. It jarred his brainpan.

Dempsey sent one back. It made Lionel think the hospital was a midway merry-go-round. Dempsey wasn't trying to hurt Lionel. He just hit him hard enough to teach him not to get fresh with the champion.

After three rounds the match ended. The two fighters shook hands. All the patients went back to their rooms. Then Dempsey and Lionel went from room to room. They gave autographs and together they cheered up the patients who had watched two champions meet in the ring.

7 An Unstoppable Force

After his Grey Cup victory, Lionel was once again offered a pro hockey contract. This time, Leo Dandurand of the Montreal Canadiens offered Lionel a $5,000 contract and a business in Montreal.

The Toronto Maple Leafs baseball club also tried to sign Lionel to a pro contract.

He turned down all offers.

People started to wonder how Lionel could turn down all the money offered him. As an amateur he should not have been paid to play sports. People started to doubt Lionel's amateur status.

Public opinion turned against Lionel. He and friend Billy Burch were accused of throwing an Aura Lee senior hockey game. It was said they were given money to play poorly to change the outcome of the game.

Hockey Star

Like Lionel Conacher, Billy Burch played football and lacrosse as well as hockey as an amateur. He turned pro as a hockey player in 1922. By the end of the season he was a member of the NHL's Hamilton Tigers. During his career he won the Hart Trophy as league MVP. He also won the Lady Byng Trophy as the NHL's most sportsmanlike player. He played with the New York Americans and finished his career with the Chicago Black Hawks. His hockey career ended with a broken leg. He is a member of the Hockey Hall of Fame.

The charges against Lionel were looked into. The Amateur Athletic Union of Canada found that Lionel had never broken the amateur code. The charges against him were dismissed, but not forgotten.

Lionel was made captain of the Argonauts before the 1922 football season. He was to bring home another Grey Cup.

The Argonauts started the season in spectacular fashion. They defeated the Montreal Winged Wheelers by a score of 20–0. Lionel was the star of the game.

"Lionel Conacher stood out like a mountain in the wilderness and his game was just about the best that he has ever played," wrote the *Globe*. "Single-handed, he provided too much for the Winged Wheelers, rushing no less than 227 yards himself."

Next, it would be another one-sided game against the Ottawa Rough Riders.

Lionel earned his new nickname, the Big Train. He ran through opposition tacklers like a locomotive steaming down the tracks.

Ottawa tackled Conacher hard and savagely. They tried every legal means to stop him. Every time he came up smiling and grabbed the ball. He would then start battering his way through the Ottawa defence.

In the second half, Lionel scored a touchdown and gave the pass for another. Twenty-yard rushes were mere walks for the big fellow. In most games, he took 40- to 60-yard rushes down the field. One of his gallops was a 70-yard sprint through a line of tacklers.

"Conacher — that's all. Those words adequately described the cause of Argos victory over Ottawa. The score was 28–1," wrote the *Star*. "Five thousand people saw an exhibition of individual playing that stamps the 22-year-old half-back as the greatest that ever stood on the Ottawa gridiron."

The Argos finished the regular season

undefeated. They won the Big Four Inter-provincial championship. It was clear that they owed their record to the great play of Lionel Conacher. In six regular season games, Conacher rushed for 950 yards. Without him, his team might not have won all those games.

The first round of the Eastern playoffs pitted the Argos against ORFU champion Parkdale. It was a Argonauts blowout; they won 20–1.

In the Eastern final, the Argonauts faced Queen's University. There was a great demand for tickets. It was the most important game of the year. Lionel knew that, and it changed him. He was an athlete who usually fed off excitement. But on this game day he was nervous.

Lionel went to the game under a lot of strain. He knew he was the hub of the game. The eyes of 17,000 people would be focused on him. If Queen's could stop him, they would win.

He did not arrive at the stadium until 15 minutes before the game was to start. He knew his raw nerves would not allow him to simply dress and wait.

In the dressing room, he climbed into his mud-encrusted armour. The instant he tied his last shoelace, he yelled out, "Come on, boys, let's go." And he got up and led the team to the field.

Outside, he nervously put on his cap. It didn't feel right, so he threw if off. As he stood waiting, he couldn't stop moving his hands from hips to thighs. He had a hard time waiting for the crucial contest to begin.

"No player of the past or present was asked to perform a more difficult feat than that demanded of Conacher on Saturday," wrote the *Globe*.

The Queen's squad was drilled in practice to stomp on the Argos star. They were themselves a mighty team. But they had to play mighty football to defeat the 1921 champion.

The opening kick came to Lionel. It looked like he would catch it, but he fumbled the ball. Queen's recovered it. On the next play, they scored the first point of the game.

"That shook the morale of the Argos more than the general public knew," wrote the *Star*. "That fumble cost the Argos more than the measly point."

Lionel had shown weakness. His teammates all knew how nervous he had been starting the game. A shiver of fear ran through the team. Lionel might not be the Big Train on this day.

After the first quarter, Queen's was winning 4–3. In the second quarter, Lionel fumbled another ball. His opponents recovered it and scored a touchdown. Queen's led 9–3.

"Many of the spectators were inclined to criticize him, but he did not deserve it," wrote the *Globe*. "Keyed up to the highest pitch of his career, Conacher felt the weight of the burden that he carried and in trying to do super human things he found after all a man can reach his limitations."

To the Argos relief, Lionel became the Big Train again in the second half. He didn't make any costly mistakes and ran with the ball. But every time he rushed there were four Queen's players rushing to tackle him. He ended up scoring six points against these tough opponents.

Queen's won the game 12–11. They would go on to win the Grey Cup against another Edmonton team.

After the game, some people blamed Lionel for the loss. But it was obvious he didn't have a very good team around him. When he had a bad game, they all did, especially against a strong team like Queen's.

"If he had not played, the Argos would have been swamped," wrote Lou Marsh of the *Star*.

Unfortunately, people took their criticism a step further. Since Lionel didn't play like the Big Train people expected, some thought he had thrown the game.

People who knew Lionel thought this charge was silly. Lionel believed in playing a hard game. He refused to accept defeat.

Even though the accusations were not true, they hurt Lionel. He didn't fill his regular defence spot on the Aura Lee senior team during the 1922–23 season. Instead, he played intermediate hockey for a North Toronto team.

For that winter Lionel disappeared from the Toronto sports scene.

8 Leaving Home

Opportunity knocked on Lionel's door in the summer of 1923. It was not in the form of another pro offer. Instead, an amateur hockey team in Pittsburgh, Pennsylvania, wanted him.

Former Toronto resident Roy Schooley was the manager of Pittsburgh's Duquesne Gardens hockey rink. He also owned the Pittsburgh Yellow Jackets amateur hockey club. The team played in the United States Amateur Hockey Association (USAHA).

Schooley was impressed with Lionel's ability to fill buildings in Canada. He saw that people came to sporting events just to see him. A few times he brought Lionel's Aura Lee club to Pittsburgh to play local teams. He even had Lionel referee games at Duquesne Gardens. The Pittsburgh fans loved to watch Lionel.

Lionel started to realize that over time the wear and tear of sport would slow him down. He needed something the Toronto sports scene couldn't offer. He had turned down many pro offers that didn't feel right to him. But the Pittsburgh offer was different.

In Pittsburgh he was offered a chance to play amateur hockey. He would have an insurance business set up for him, so he could make money when not playing sports. The hockey team would pay his tuition at a university where he could improve his education. At the school he could play for the football team. More important to Lionel was the guarantee that his amateur status in Canada would be protected. He could still play amateur baseball and lacrosse in Toronto during the summer.

Lionel accepted Schooley's offer. But he wouldn't be going to Pittsburgh alone. Many of Lionel's teammates from various hockey clubs followed him south. They would call this their Pittsburgh Adventure. The list of players included Harold Cotton, Duke McCurry, and goalie Roy Worters.

"Lionel made me go," said Worters about going to Pittsburgh. "I was fed up with hockey after the 1922–23 season. I wasn't going to play anymore. Then one day I'm playing a ball game against him. He came over to me and said, 'You're going to Pittsburgh with me next winter.' I said, 'Oh no, I'm not.' He said, 'Oh yes, you are.' So I went to Pittsburgh."

When the Yellow Jackets were not playing hockey, they would go to school or work day jobs. Lionel and Harold studied at Bellefonte Academy, while Duke McCurry and Paddy Sullivan were in dental school. Goalie Roy Worters and Tex White worked at the Duquesne Gardens box office. All the other players had regular jobs.

Old Rubberlegs

Harold Cotton, nicknamed Old Rubberlegs, played for 12 years in the NHL. After playing in Pittsburgh for four years, Cotton moved on to the Toronto Maple Leafs. His best season was 1929–30, when he scored 21 goals. Cotton played 500 NHL games, scoring 101 goals and 204 points. Later he became a coach and scout. He was credited with discovering a young defenceman named Bobby Orr.

Leaving to go to Pittsburgh wasn't the only change in Lionel's life. On September 23, 1923, he married Dorothy Kennedy.

At Bellefonte Academy Lionel instantly

The Hillcrest baseball club, along with numerous other Toronto area sports fans, were sad to see Lionel go to Pittsburgh. Here Lionel was showing off the handbag and wreath given to him by the club.

became the star of the football team. He played alongside Toronto friend Harold Cotton.

In one of his first games for Bellefonte, Lionel single-handedly defeated St. Francis College. In the first quarter, Lionel made three touchdowns. The St. Francis players were unable to stop him. On each of the three touchdowns he ran at least half the length of the field.

Lionel sat the whole third quarter. He got back into the game in the last quarter, and scored his fourth touchdown. Bellefonte beat St. Francis 45–0.

In a game against Carnegie Tech, Cotton and Lionel showed how football was played in Canada. They engineered what was probably the first lateral pass seen in Pennsylvania. At one point, Carnegie Tech was forced to punt the ball to Bellefonte. Cotton caught the ball. He ran a few steps to draw opposition tacklers toward him. When they got close, he flipped a lateral pass to Conacher. Lionel caught the ball and charged 60 yards for a touchdown.

The Tech players and coaches screamed at the Canadian players. They reached for their rule books. They didn't think lateral passes were allowed. They learned the play was perfectly legal. The Americans had just never seen it done before that day.

After Bellefonte won the game 40–0, Lionel and Cotton attended their first Pittsburgh hockey practice.

"Conacher was probably the greatest athlete I ever coached in football or any other form of athletics," said Carl Snavely, Lionel's football coach at Bellefonte. "He possessed all the qualities of speed, skill, dexterity, aggressiveness, self-control, and the various attributes that are required for superiority in the American game of football. In less than one season Conacher,

Pittsburgh Skating Palace

Duquesne Gardens, home ice for the Yellow Jackets, was built in 1890 to store streetcars. It was converted to a skating rink in 1896 and hockey was played there starting in 1899. It was called the Largest and Most Beautiful Skating Palace in the World. It was demolished in 1956.

who had never seen the American game played, became one of the outstanding prep school players of all time."

Lionel played football until the hockey season started. Hockey was his primary reason for being there.

He was an outstanding football player at Bellefonte. But he became a superstar Pittsburgh attraction as a hockey player. When Lionel and his Canadian teammates visited other cities they were called the Wonder Team. Lionel was called Canada's Wonder Athlete.

Lionel was the captain of the Yellow Jackets. In the first game of the season, he thrilled fans by scoring three goals. In the final game of regular season play, a Pittsburgh paper proclaimed Lionel to be "Pittsburgh's mighty man of valor."

The USAHA was the top hockey league in the United States. The Pittsburgh Yellow Jackets were the top team in the league. They won the national championship of 1923–24.

Lionel was the star of the team. He scored 28 goals in 29 games. He was the league's top scorer with 87 points. Playing defence, he provided a part of Pittsburgh's noted stonewall defence.

Pittsburgh hockey fans loved Lionel and the hockey championship he brought to the city. They were so happy they bought him a new car.

It seemed nothing could stop the Big Train in Pittsburgh.

The 1924 football season had Lionel star for the Duquesne University football team. And the Yellow Jackets were the 1924–25 USAHA national champions.

But Lionel's career high didn't last long. After the 1924–25 season the USAHA officially folded. Lionel's team found itself without a league to play in. He would have to make some changes himself.

9 Battle for Control

Before 1924, the NHL was made up of four teams: the Toronto St. Pats, Montreal Canadiens, Hamilton Tigers, and Ottawa Senators. In 1924, the Boston Bruins became the first American club, and the Montreal Maroons became the second club in that city.

New York City's Madison Square Garden had been built to house boxing and wrestling matches. After watching a hockey game, the owner put ice in the

Garden so he could have his own NHL hockey team. In 1925 the Hamilton club was moved to New York. They would be called the New York Americans.

When the USAHA folded and the Pittsburgh Yellow Jackets didn't have a league to play in, team owner Roy Schooley was having financial troubles. He sold the team to attorney James F. Callahan. The new owner had big plans for the club.

There were rumours Pittsburgh would become the third American NHL club. People wondered if Lionel would finally turn pro.

Lionel had turned down every pro offer. But times were changing for the sports star. He was getting older. He was moving past his peak years as an athlete. He was married and would soon have a family to support. He still supported his parents in Toronto.

Birthplace of Pro Hockey

The Western Pennsylvania Hockey League, with all Pittsburgh-based teams, was the first pro hockey league. It operated from 1901 to 1904. The first inter-city pro league, based in Pittsburgh, was the International Hockey League (IHL), which operated from 1904 to 1907. The IHL team based in Sault Ste. Marie, Ontario, was Canada's first pro hockey team.

His favourite sport was football, but there was no pro league in Canada. If he signed a pro contract, it would end his career as an amateur. He would not only have to give up playing football, but also baseball and lacrosse. It was a tough decision.

As a popular young athlete, Lionel had been wanted by many Toronto teams. His name would be enough to fill the stands with spectators. Pro hockey teams had tried to sign him for his popularity and not his hockey skills. Lionel knew he hadn't been ready to be a pro hockey player.

By 1925 he knew he was ready as an athlete to turn pro as a hockey player. Over the years he had worked hard at improving his hockey skills. He had developed into a star hockey player. He knew turning pro offered him the greatest opportunity for a lengthy paying career.

The NHL head office was in Montreal. The new Pittsburgh team owners planned to go there in early November 1925 to arrange entry into the league. Lionel was assured a spot on the team. But he had one last wish before he turned pro in the fall of 1925.

"I sure would like to play one more game for my old club, the Argos," said Lionel, who had not played Canadian football since the fall of 1922.

One day Lionel surprised the Argonauts. He turned up at their practice field. He put on his gear and practiced with the club.

"If Conacher plays for Argos Saturday it will make a difference between a crowd of 2,000 and a crowd of 7,000," wrote the *Star*. "The boys would certainly like to see the big fellow play once more."

Lionel planned to play for the Argos against the Montreal Winged Wheelers. It would be his last game as an amateur athlete.

There were thousands of fans who wanted to see Lionel play one more time. The Argos wanted Lionel to play. But Montreal didn't. They argued that he no longer had amateur status. They believed he had already signed a pro hockey contract. If Lionel played, Montreal would walk off the field.

Even though Lionel loved football, he

was a true sportsman. If he played, the Argos would lose the game by default. He didn't want that. His last amateur wish was put aside. He never played for the Argos again.

On November 7, 1925, Pittsburgh became the third American city with an NHL team. The name Yellow Jackets was dropped. They were named the Pittsburgh Pirates, just like the baseball team. Their jerseys were bright yellow with black stripes and a large *P* on the front.

Four days later, Lionel signed a three-year pro contract with the club. He would be paid $7,500 per year, making him the highest paid player in the NHL at the time.

The entire Yellow Jackets lineup had turned professional. It was a team Lionel had put together over two years. He thought he should manage the new club. Other people thought that too.

"That squad of Yellow Jackets would not have been in the NHL this season if it had not been for Conacher," wrote the *Star*, knowing his participation had helped Pittsburgh land an NHL team. The paper also knew the importance of Lionel on the ice: "He has been the backbone of the team both defensively and offensively."

But it was not to be. The club passed on Lionel as manager. They picked Odie Cleghorn to manage the team. Cleghorn would also play for the team. He was the only non-Yellow Jacket to join the team. Most of the players were not happy with the club's decision. If there was to be a player-manager, why not Conacher?

The Pirates' first game was against the Boston Bruins. Lionel scored the first goal in Pirates history. The game also resulted in the team's first victory.

Lionel played his best hockey at the beginning of the season. He earned great praise from the media. But by the end of the regular season, his play had declined. It was rumoured that the reason was that Lionel could not cooperate with Cleghorn.

Cleghorn managed his team differently from most. He played with three lines instead of two. He switched his players on the fly, while other teams switched players only when they got tired. This is how hockey is played now, but it was new back then. The players got less ice time. They didn't like the new game plan.

The combination of Cleghorn's tactics and denying the manager position to Lionel caused trouble on the team. Lionel's teammates were loyal to him. It was predicted Cleghorn would not be with Pittsburgh another season. But the team's management liked Cleghorn. He led the team to the playoffs in their first season.

All that didn't matter to Lionel. He

didn't like how he was being treated. If it didn't change by the next season, he wanted out of Pittsburgh.

The Pain in Conacher's Side

Odie Cleghorn played ten seasons in the NHL. He started his career with the Montreal Canadiens. He was the Pittsburgh Pirates' player-coach for three seasons. His brother Sprague, who had also been a pro hockey player, died of injuries following a car accident in 1956. They were very close. A few hours later Odie was found dead in bed. Some said he died because of the stress of his brother's death.

10 A New Start

The 1926–27 season brought changes to the NHL. The league expanded again, adding the New York Rangers, Chicago Black Hawks, and Detroit Cougars.

In Pittsburgh, Odie Cleghorn was still the player-manager of the Pirates. Lionel talked the team's owners into trading him to the New York Americans.

Lionel would be reunited with an old friend wearing the red, white, and blue uniform of the Americans. Billy Burch was

Off the Ice

The summer of 1926 Lionel played three games of pro baseball as an outfielder for the Toronto Maple Leafs of the International League. He hadn't played baseball since 1922. In 1927, Lionel became an assistant football coach at Rutgers University in New Jersey.

the captain and offensive star of the team. In New York, Lionel would find a new influence on his career, Tommy Gorman, the manager of the Americans.

Gorman was originally from Ottawa. He never played hockey, but was a keen scout of hockey talent. In 1917 he was named the manager of the NHL's Ottawa Senators. In Ottawa he put together teams that won the Stanley Cup in 1920, 1921, and 1923. The Americans were looking for that same success.

The trade renewed Lionel. He became the defensive star of the Americans. He was not restrained as he had been by Cleghorn's system.

That first season as an American he was second only to Billy Burch in scoring. These two players were the only bright spots on the team, and the Americans lost more games than they won. They missed the playoffs with a 17-25-2 record.

During his first season with New York, Lionel learned a hard lesson when he visited his hometown of Toronto. On February 17, 1927, Lionel's Americans were playing the Toronto St. Pats. Most of the Americans lineup were players from Toronto. They were hometown boys. Lionel was Toronto's greatest athlete, but the hockey fans booed him. Lionel let the fans' reaction get to him.

"Conacher is very foolish to let these ranting and ravings of a few flatheads hurt

The line-up of the 1928–29 New York Americans.

him, for every rat who boos him here, there are a hundred who look upon him as a fine upstanding athlete who possesses and exhibits real sportsmanship on all occasions," wrote Lou Marsh of the *Toronto Star*.

The Americans management changed during the off-season. Former player Shorty Green replaced Gorman.

This change didn't help the Americans. Lionel and Burch were still their top players. The rest of the team were duds. They finished last in their division and again missed the playoffs, this time with even fewer wins and a 11-27-6 record. Across the city of New York, the New York Rangers became the first American team to win the Stanley Cup.

Tommy Gorman was brought back to the Americans before the 1928–29 season. He had to rebuild the team to be winners. Lionel helped out by suggesting some of his Toronto hockey friends. Gorman was happy to take Lionel's advice.

"Lionel Conacher is not only one of the greatest players in hockey, but he is largely responsible for the success of the Americans this winter," said Gorman "I have consulted 'Connie' in every move and his advice has always proved invaluable. The Toronto boys on the American team are very popular in New York this winter."

Lionel and Burch were two of the remaining Americans from the previous season. Most of the team was let go. One of the key signings was Pittsburgh goalie Roy Worters.

Roy Worters was the shortest player, at 160 cm (5 feet, 3 inches), to ever play in the NHL. He would go on to become a member of the Hockey Hall of Fame.

"Lionel was instrumental in getting me to New York with him," said Worters. "I don't know how he did it, but he must have said 'There's the fellow we want,' and they'd have to do something about it."

The new-look Americans had their best season since becoming a franchise in 1925. They finished second in their division with a 19-13-2 record.

The first round of the playoffs was an all-New-York-City affair — Americans vs. Rangers. The series would be close. The first game ended in a 0–0 tie. The Rangers squeaked one goal past Worters to win the second game 1–0. That single goal was all the Rangers needed to go to the next level. The Americans' season was done.

Roy Worters was a big reason for the team's success that season. He was awarded the Hart Trophy, the first goalie to be named league MVP. Lionel was also a factor and was seventh in MVP voting.

Lionel would finally get his hockey wish before the 1929–30 season. Gorman left the Americans to manage a racetrack in Mexico. Lionel became the player-manager of the Americans. To play on and manage the same team — that was what he'd wanted back in Pittsburgh. It was to be the worst move in his career.

The Americans had a rough start to the 1929–30 season. After five games they had only one victory.

On December 3, 1929, the Americans faced the Toronto Maple Leafs. On the Leafs was an exciting new rookie, Lionel's younger brother Charlie. Lionel had helped Charlie sign a two-year contract worth $20,000 with their hometown team.

Charlie Conacher was one of the most feared goal scorers in NHL history. He was a member of the Kid Line that included Busher Jackson and Joe Primeau.

It was the first game between the two brothers. Unfortunately, Lionel's play was slipping.

"Big Train Conacher looked the best of a bad collection," wrote the *Star*. "His management duties have worn him to a frizzle and he looked no more like the Lionel Conacher of old. He was fair defensively, but his offensive work was flat. He only made two real rushes all night."

"Amazing Amerks — Not," wrote another newspaper.

By the end of the season Lionel benched himself. He was not playing NHL-calibre hockey.

The Americans had their worst season yet. They finished last overall, with a 14-25-5 record. Lionel was not a success as a manager or as a player that year.

11 Picking Up the Pieces

Before the 1930–31 hockey season started, Lionel was traded to the Montreal Maroons. The Maroons saw Lionel as an important addition to the team.

"The hefty defenseman should add considerable weight to the Maroons defense which, previous to Conacher's signing, was the weak spot on the team," wrote the *Star*.

Instead of saving the team, Lionel turned into a big disappointment. "The

Maroons recognized that he'd slowed to a walk, asked waivers on him. Meaning that any club in the NHL could claim his services for $10,000," wrote the *Star*. "Significant of his decline, there were no takers."

"At that time I had been in the NHL for four years, only to find myself an unwanted veteran," said Lionel.

Some people thought his career had been at an end in New York. In Montreal it looked like it was true.

During Lionel's stay in New York City, his fondness for whisky got out of control. The more he drank, the worse his game became. Some said he drank two bottles of hard liquor each day. That was highly unlikely. But his brother Charlie said Lionel was like the soft drink slogan, trying to "Drink Canada Dry."

Lionel took this problem with him to Montreal. His level of play fell even more.

Lionel as a Montreal Maroon. Most of his best seasons came as a Maroon.

By the early 1930s, the Great Depression had hit North America. The rich economy of the 1920s started a downward spiral. It seemed like it couldn't get worse. As time went by, it did.

Lionel knew what poverty felt like. He had grown up poor. He didn't want to go back to that life.

People were losing their jobs daily. Lionel was a high paid sports star who might lose his job. He didn't know anything else. He had to do something to keep his job.

Keeping his job became even more important to Lionel when he became a father. On November 25, 1930, daughter Constance was born. Constance would be the key to Lionel's return as a star athlete. He promised his wife that things would be different. Lionel had realized that his career was finished unless things changed.

The first step was to quit drinking. Lionel had a constant craving for alcohol. It took a great effort to resist the urge to drink. He would drink pots of tea and smoke a pipe to curb his need for alcohol.

Journalist Andy O'Brien recalled, "I used to watch him drink nine Cokes and eat a box of chocolates before going to bed, but he licked the craving."

Lionel had to fill his days with activities to keep his mind off drinking. He played golf. He went to movies, but he could never sit through a whole show. His body wouldn't let him.

Hard Times

The Great Depression was hard on the NHL. Many clubs moved and then dropped out of the league. The Pittsburgh Pirates became the Philadelphia Quakers, but after one season that team folded. The Ottawa Senators club became the St. Louis Eagles, and then folded after a couple of seasons. The Detroit Cougars didn't fold; they just changed their name to Falcons and then Red Wings.

While he was trying to break the hold drink had on him, he caught pneumonia. After that he was hospitalized to remove a painful growth.

The whole ordeal was hard on Lionel's body. Now he had to become an athlete again. He had to build up his skills and confidence. He drove himself hard to become the athlete he once had been.

"It was in 1930 that I experienced my hardest battle as an athlete," said Lionel, "getting out of the broken-down has-been rut."

When he first joined the Maroons he was not in good shape. When he didn't play well, the fans rebelled against him. He was benched. Team manager Dunc Munro had to play in his spot.

When Johnny Gallagher on defence broke his hand, the Maroons were in deep trouble. They couldn't get by without two defence players. Lionel asked for a second chance. The team let him come back, as long as he stayed away from the bottle.

Lionel's first game back was against the Montreal Canadiens. He gave an outstanding performance. Through determination and hard work, he changed the jeers of the crowd to cheers.

Late in the season, the Maroons played the Toronto Maple Leafs. Lionel showed his hometown crowd he was back in his old form.

"One thing that tickled Toronto fans was to see Big Train showing some of his old time form," wrote Lou Marsh of the *Star*. "Here is one chap who is pulling for the boy to finish his comeback in a blaze of glory."

Lionel's play improved as the season went on. He played every game. There wasn't any more talk of getting rid of him. The Maroons club found itself fighting for a playoff berth. And some were saying it was because of Lionel.

"Montreal's dramatic run for play-off berth must be credited to Lionel," wrote the *Star*. The Maroons finished the season with a 20–18–6 record. Even though the Maroons were eliminated in the first round of the playoffs, Lionel's hockey comeback had been a success.

12 Youth Revisited

Lacrosse is a game halfway between hockey and football. It is a physical game. It was a sport that made the most of Lionel's talent for sports. Next to football, it was his favourite sport.

Lionel played the forward position in lacrosse. Just like in football, he used swerving rushes down the field. He pressed his stick against his body, cradled the ball in its netting, and ploughed through the defence.

Lionel's progress through lacrosse mirrored his football career. He had started playing lacrosse as a teenager. By 1920, he was a leading player in the game. By 1923 he was the star attraction people paid to see. But Lionel stopped playing lacrosse when he turned to pro hockey.

Fan interest in lacrosse dropped as other sports grew in popularity. People found baseball and football more exciting to watch.

Lacrosse supporters wanted to make the sport popular again. They thought lacrosse could be played indoors in hockey arenas in the off-season. On this smaller surface, lacrosse would be a much faster game. It could be as exciting as hockey. This new indoor game would be called box lacrosse. The best part was that the hockey off-season left rinks and players available to play in the summer.

A four-team pro league was formed in

1931. It was called the International Indoor Professional Lacrosse League. There would be three NHL-owned teams: the Montreal Canadiens, Montreal Maroons, and Toronto Maple Leafs. The fourth team was based in Cornwall.

The league gave pro athletes the chance to play another sport. Lacrosse was a favourite sport for many athletes. Like Lionel, they all had to give it up when they turned pro.

Lionel missed playing lacrosse. So he joined the Montreal Maroons club. Many of his NHL teammates were also on the team.

One newspaper wrote that, "seeing Conacher in action in lacrosse is alone worth the price of admission."

The inaugural game of the league was between the Montreal rivals. Most fans were doubtful of how the game would turn out.

"I never thought a lacrosse game could be so fast and neither did the crowd. They came down there prepared to sit back and give it the hee-haw if it wasn't good," wrote the *Star*. "Before the game had been underway two minutes the fans were up on their hind legs yelling their heads off and hurling taunts at each other as their favorites alternately took and lost the lead."

The Maroons won 9–7.

If Lionel ever stopped being called Big Train, he earned back the nickname playing lacrosse against the Toronto Maple Leafs.

"Conacher came to his home city rated as being slightly inferior to his teammate Nels Stewart. He had something to strive for and he came through with flying colors. Throughout the game voices could be heard all over the Arena, 'watch Conacher!'" wrote the *Globe*.

A crowd of 4,200 people watched the

Leafs defeat the Maroons 9–7. Even though his team lost, Lionel was the star of the game. He scored six goals and assisted on another.

"Conacher is the greatest of them all," said one player.

Former lacrosse great Joe Lally of Cornwall had even greater things to say. "Lionel is a superman and above all a gentleman. Why, time after time, three or four men piled on him. And they tried to get him in every way, but he paid no attention to the fouls and the abuse. He went right on playing the game."

During the season, the Maple Leafs held a Lionel Conacher Night. People in Toronto wanted to celebrate the renewed career of their own great athlete.

"There was a time when certain Toronto fans criticized Conacher unmercifully and the latter resented such attacks. Now, however, he realized that it was all a mistake, just the ups and downs of sport. Last night's festivities wiped misunderstanding aside," wrote the *Globe*. "'The Big Train' was cheered to the echo, a tribute that he has long been entitled to in his home city."

Lionel would go on to score three goals in a Maroons 10–7 defeat that night.

The Maroons lacrosse team did not make the championship final that summer. It was played out between the Canadiens and Maple Leafs. But Lionel was the league's powerhouse. He won the scoring title with 107 points. His nearest rival had only 56 points.

Lionel decided not to play lacrosse in the summer of 1932. The game was too rough on his body. He said it was a young man's game. Instead, he announced that he would take on pro wrestling. He thought he had only so many years left to make a living as a pro athlete. Wrestling was another way to add to his income.

A crowd of 5,500 people filled Toronto's Arena Garden to watch Lionel's first wrestling match. Two local radio stations aired Lionel's bout with ring veteran Karl Pospesheil. The crowd seemed to be cheering for Lionel.

Pospesheil tossed Lionel high in the air, but Conacher was not hurt. On one occasion, Lionel was slammed viciously to the mat. Lionel came back with his own moves. He put Karl in a painful scissor hold. He added extra action with flying tackles.

Lionel won his first wrestling match. Over the summer he travelled all over Ontario and Quebec to wrestle. He won all 26 matches he wrestled in. After many of his matches he was given a standing ovation.

Lionel's wrestling adventure ended when he hurt his elbow. He decided hockey was easier on his body. He returned to the Maroons lineup in the fall of 1932.

In his amateur days, Lionel changed sports by the season. In his thirties, he was doing his best to repeat that feat as a pro. People wondered what new pro sport he would take up next.

Box Lacrosse Today

The International Lacrosse League only lasted two seasons. But it started a new form of the sport that is still being played today. Many pro box lacrosse leagues formed in the past but never lasted more than a few seasons. The most successful league is the one currently in operation. The National Lacrosse League was formed in 1987. Three of its twelve teams are Canadian: the Toronto Rock, Calgary Roughnecks, and Edmonton Rush. More than two-thirds of the players in the league are from Canada.

13 Football Dreams Come True

As Lionel got older he became a better hockey defenceman. The 1932–33 season was his best yet. At 32 years of age he was one of the best in the NHL. He had his highest NHL point total ever — 28 points, with 7 goals and 21 assists. He was also named to the NHL's Second All-Star team.

Lionel was at an age when most players are in their slow decline into retirement. But Lionel seemed like a rookie player ready to show the league how well he could play.

At one point Lionel was offered a football coaching position with the Montreal Winged Wheelers. The club was part of the Big Four football league he once played in. They saw him as an asset because of his coaching experience at Rutgers University.

In Montreal, they thought he would jump at the chance to get back into football. But Lionel turned down the offer. He was already signed to play other paying sports.

Football was Lionel's favourite sport, and it was always in his thoughts. Lionel didn't play lacrosse or wrestle in the summer of 1933. Instead he organized something new to Canada. He put together the country's first pro football team.

Lionel signed a contract with a food company called Crosse and Blackwell to

Lionel liked to show people how to kick farther. Most people watched just to see Lionel in action.

sponsor the new football team. The team would be called the Crosse and Blackwell Chefs.

The team would play pro clubs from Rochester and Buffalo in New York State. Lionel used his own reputation to advertise the games. For the fans it was a chance to see the Big Train in action again.

The opening game would be on Canadian Thanksgiving Day, 1933. Lionel had the summer to put together a team. Since football was not a pro sport in Canada, his players were former amateur athletes who had turned pro in other sports to make a living. A lot of the players he picked for the team were pro wrestlers.

Former hockey teammate Duke McCurry signed to play. For a bit of fun, Lionel's brother Charlie signed up. He was the team's quarterback, even though he had never played senior football.

The team would centre on the Big Train. He was the star. Some people had doubts about Lionel. It was not known how he would perform. He had not played

Bringing Together Canadian Football

In 1955, the Inter-provincial Union, or Big Four, played off against the Western Canadian Rugby Football Union for the Grey Cup in an all-pro matchup. The Big Four were the Toronto Argonauts, Hamilton Tiger-Cats, Ottawa Rough Riders, and Montreal Alouettes. The Western teams were the Edmonton Eskimos, Saskatchewan Roughriders, Winnipeg Blue Bombers, BC Lions, and Calgary Stampeders. In 1956 they formed the Canadian Football Council, which became the Canadian Football League in 1958.

football for nine years.

The Chefs' first game was against the Rochester Arpeakos. Toronto's Maple Leaf Stadium sold 13,000 seats for the game. As it was when he was an Argo, Lionel was the focus of all eyes.

The aging star did not disappoint. Lionel was the best man on the field. The Big Train was in every play.

"Lionel was the running, kicking, catching, grid general of old," wrote the *Star*. "The fans applauded the rest of the boys. But, for Lionel they stood up on their hind legs and screamed."

Lionel ran with the ball, weaving his way through his opponents. He scored the first touchdown of the game as he rushed the ball 20 yards. Later, he sprinted the ball 75 yards for his second touchdown.

"The second Chefs score brought the crowd to its feet howling," wrote the *Star*. "Tricky footwork left Arpeakos tacklers groveling in the sod to right and left as the Big Train galloped down the south side of the field and over the line."

In the dying moments of the game, Lionel received the ball from a teammate. He ran it down the field 20 yards and then flipped it to Duke McCurry. The Duke took it the rest of the way for a touchdown.

Even against Lionel's amazing play, Rochester won the game 18–15. Lionel was an important factor in all of Toronto's fifteen points. The *Toronto Star* headline read, "Lionel Conacher Shines Once More as Big Train."

"For younger generations the game was a great opportunity to learn just what their parents have been talking about when they recall the exploits of the Big Train on the gridiron," wrote the *Star*.

The second game of the season was played in Rochester. The Arpeakos won 12–6.

A victory for the Chefs finally came in the third and final game of the season. The Chefs defeated a Buffalo pro squad 18–0. It was a hometown win played at Maple Leaf Stadium. Lionel continued to be the

Big Train of old, scoring 13 points.

The pro football experiment continued in the fall of 1934. The Toronto club changed sponsors to the Wrigley Gum Company. The team's name was changed to the Wrigley Aromints.

"The new team will be much stronger than were the Chefs, pioneers in local professional rank," said Lionel. The new

Birth of Pro American Football

Pro football in the United States can be traced back to 1892, when one player was paid to play in a game for the Allegheny Athletic Association team against the Pittsburgh Athletic Club. The first pro league was the Ohio League formed in 1903. In 1920, the American Professional Football Association was formed. Two years later it changed its name to the National Football League (NFL).

team was a collection of boxers, wrestlers, hockey players, doctors, and dentists.

The Aromints won all three of their games against the Rochester and Buffalo pro teams.

Once the season was over, Lionel's football career ended. He was 34 years old. The grind of football was too hard on his body.

Lionel was happy to relive his past glories on the football field. Younger fans got to see the Big Train firsthand. Older people were reminded of a time when he was the king of Canadian football.

Lionel needed to use his summers to recover from the previous season of hockey. Spending time with his family and fishing trips with friends renewed him for the upcoming season. Lionel was still looking to play hockey for many years.

14 His Finest Season

In 1933, the Chicago Black Hawks brought Tommy Gorman back to the NHL. Team owner Major Frederic McLaughlin needed somebody to rebuild his club after the disaster of the 1932–33 season. They had finished last in their division with a 16-20-12 record.

Gorman wanted to build his team around goalie Charlie Gardiner and Lionel Conacher on defence. But Conacher was still a Montreal Maroon. Gorman acquired

Lionel through a trade.

Lionel was an older player at 33 years of age. He didn't have the speed younger players had. After all his body had gone through in many years of sport, he was lucky he could even skate. His knees were shot. To be able to skate a full game he had to wrap them in tape.

Lionel fought against his body's decline, determined to win.

"I'll always remember the time when I never left the ice in four games. We won two and tied two," said Lionel.

What Lionel had over younger players was smarts. He could develop the play to stop his opponents. He knew how to play the angle. When an opponent sped into his zone he could keep himself between the goal and the forward trying to pass him. He would push the forward into the corner and take the puck away.

Like in his football days, Lionel could get

Lionel's body took a beating after playing so many years of sports.

rough. Sometimes opposing players would get under his skin. He usually kept his temper. But he lost it when pushed too far.

Lionel's temper was seen in a game against the New York Rangers. He battled the Rangers players singly and in groups. Next he made a few swings at taunting fans. He was still offering to battle anybody and everybody in the house when the police took him away. It took a group of police to get Lionel into the dressing room.

People looked forward to a meeting on ice between the two brothers, Lionel and Charlie. The most important person in the stands would be their mother.

"To my parents hockey meant that their boys had made good. I remember that Mother loved to go to the Garden when her sons were playing. She'd sit there with Dad and she'd look around at the tremendous crowd of thousands and she'd say to Dad, 'Imagine, Ben, all these people are cheering our boys,'" said Charlie. "Mother always took the most pride in

Hockey's Conachers

Charlie Conacher was nine years younger than Lionel. His nickname was the Big Bomber. Five times in six years, Charlie led or tied for the NHL scoring title. He was elected to both the Hockey Hall of Fame and the Canadian Sports Hall of Fame. The Hockey News ranked Charlie Conacher 36th in their 100 Greatest Players list. Roy Conacher was Lionel's youngest brother. He was the third Conacher brother to win the Memorial Cup. In his rookie season with Boston he topped the league in goals scored. He became the third Conacher brother elected to the Hockey Hall of Fame.

our success."

By the end of the regular season, Black Hawks manager Tommy Gorman looked like a miracle worker. He had changed a last-place team into a winner. He added and subtracted to the lineup. He had hired on Lionel, who became their star defenceman. The 1933–34 Hawks had a 20-17-11 record. It was good enough to place second in the NHL's American division. They made it into the Stanley Cup playoffs.

The Stanley Cup quarter-finals and semi-finals were total-goal series. Whichever team scored the most goals in the two games won the series.

In the quarter-final the Hawks defeated the Montreal Canadiens 4–3. In the semi-final they defeated the Montreal Maroons 6–2.

The Black Hawks entered their first Stanley Cup final. The final series was a first for Lionel too. They would face the Detroit Red Wings in a best-of-five-games series.

The first two games were played in Detroit. More than 14,000 people packed the rink for each game.

In the first game Lionel became a star in

the offence. In his own end he grabbed the puck and rushed down the ice. He barged his way through the Detroit defence at their blue line. He finished by skating right up to Detroit goalie Wilf Cude to score with a shot to the corner. It was the first goal of the game.

"The Big Train made other rushes and his defensive work was near-perfect," wrote the *Star*.

Chicago won the first game 2–1. They followed with another 4–1 victory.

Detroit got back into the series by winning the third game in Chicago.

The fourth game became a standoff. More than 16,500 Chicago fans were on the edge of their seats wanting their team to score. Detroit goaltender Cude stopped 53 shots over three periods. Chicago goalie Gardiner made 40 saves.

The game was scoreless after three periods. It would be decided in sudden-death overtime. After 30 minutes and 5 seconds, Mush Marsh of the Black Hawks scored the winning goal.

The stadium erupted in cheers. The Black Hawks were Stanley Cup champions. The Chicago fans gave their club a ten-minute standing ovation.

It was the team Gorman built and Lionel was its foundation.

"It has taken Lionel Conacher eight years of NHL campaigning to reach these heights," wrote the *Star*. "They said Conacher's weakest sport was hockey. But he made good from the start. He definitely reached stardom with the Maroons last season. Conny's presence on the Chicago defense gave the Hawks what they needed to become Stanley Cup champions."

Lionel was considered one of the best defencemen in the NHL that season. He was named to the NHL's First All-Star team. He was also second in voting for the

Hart Trophy as league MVP.

Gorman left the Chicago club after the Stanley Cup victory. It was rumoured that Chicago gangster Al Capone ran Gorman out of town. Gorman signed on as the manager of the Montreal Maroons. He wanted Lionel to come to Montreal with him.

"I told Major McLaughlin I wanted Lionel to go with me," said Gorman. "McLaughlin wouldn't hear of it. But, Lionel told him he would shoot the puck into his own net if Chicago didn't make a deal for him. The result was one of hockey's biggest swaps involving three clubs."

Just as he did in Chicago, Gorman centred the Maroons on Lionel and their goalie. Gorman talked retired goalie Alex Connell back to the Maroons. Connell had played for Gorman in the 1920s with the Ottawa Senators. The Ottawa Fireman, as Connell was called, played an amazing year of hockey. It helped having Lionel playing in front of him.

The Maroons finished the season with a 24-19-5 record. It was good enough for second place in the Canadian division. The Maple Leafs were first in the division and overall.

In the quarter-finals the Maroons narrowly beat Chicago 1–0, scoring the only goal over two games. They had another close series in the semi-finals against the Rangers. The Maroons won that series 5–4 and earned a spot in the Stanley Cup finals.

The Stanley Cup final round was between the Maroons and the Toronto Maple Leafs. It was another duel between Lionel on defence and Charlie as the high-flying forward.

The Leafs were favourites to win. They had a strong offensive punch with the legendary Kid Line of Charlie, Joe Primeau, and Busher Jackson. They also had a very strong goalie, multi-Vezina trophy winner George Hainesworth.

But the Leafs found the Maroons were too strong defensively. Toronto's strong offence could not score any goals.

Maroons goalie Alex Connell became the hero of the series. He made save after save. This gave the Maroons' forwards a chance to take and keep the lead.

The Maroons won the first two games of the best-of-five series. When the third game was over, Connell leaned back on the crossbar and cried. But they were not tears of sorrow. The stress was over. The Maroons had won their third straight game. They had the Stanley Cup for the second time in team history.

When Lionel played for Chicago, the Montreal fans in the Millionaire End of the Forum had booed him. When he became a Maroon he vowed to turn their jeers to cheers.

"At the end of the season, he skated down to that end of the rink with the Stanley Cup held high over his head. He received one of the greatest ovations any player ever received in Montreal. That was Lionel's finest season," said Gorman.

Lionel and Gorman were a formula for success. Lionel's genius for leadership made him a great team player and a favourite with coaches. He simply refused

A Champion-Builder

After the Montreal Maroons folded in 1938, Tommy Gorman became the general manager of the Montreal Canadiens. He led them to Stanley Cup victories in 1944 and 1946. He is the only person in any sport to manage four different teams to league championships. He was inducted into the Hockey Hall of Fame in 1963.

to accept defeat.

"Conacher was the greatest hockey player I ever handled. He engineered two world hockey championships for me," said Gorman. "There'll never be another Conacher. He was Canada's greatest."

15 The End of an Era

Lionel took much punishment over his sports career. In an article in *Maclean's* magazine Lionel gave a list of his injuries.

He said he had broken his nose eight times, broken an arm and a leg, broken several bones in his hands, and cracked ten ribs. He had received a skate gash across his jugular vein that needed sixteen stitches and was inches away from killing him. A cut on his thigh had gone septic and gangrene had almost killed him. He had

had two knee operations and 650 stitches, 500 of them on his face and head area.

These were just the major injuries. Lionel said the lesser injuries included sprains, pulled ligaments, twisted muscles, black eyes, bumps, aches, and bruises.

Physical injuries slowed his body down over the years. The mental aspect of his game also got harder as time went on.

It took a lot to be the Big Train. He had to live up to the standard he had laid down in 20 years of sport. His body wanted to be in an easy chair. His brain had to tell the body it couldn't do that.

Before the start of the 1936–37 season, the *Toronto Star* made two announcements. A big picture of legendary Maple Leafs defenceman King Clancy filled the page with the news of his retirement. In an article beside it, Lionel announced his own retirement. For both players it would be their last season as pro athletes.

People thought Lionel would never retire. After 20 years they didn't know what sport would be like without him.

Lionel hadn't done any pre-season training and was tired. More than once he rested on the ice in front of the goal. When he returned to the dressing room he slumped in his seat.

Lionel admitted in his deep voice that it was, "kind of tough," in his first workout. "I've got to get my legs into shape and then I'll be OK," he told the *Toronto Star*.

"But," he grunted as he untied a skate lace, "I'll be all right by the time the league opening rolls around."

He wouldn't be the Big Train if he were ready.

Lionel didn't let his fans down. He had a great season. He was a strong defender of the Maroons net. He never hesitated to rush the puck down the ice to try to score. Once the Maroons secured a safe lead, they could not be beaten. That was Lionel's doing.

"Conacher was a raging tower of skill and fighting strength," said one newspaper.

Lionel's last pro hockey game was on April 23, 1937. He was a month away from turning 37. For more than 20 years he strived to be a great athlete. He would do anything to win. But now he was done. In 498 season NHL games he scored 80 goals and had 105 points.

Lionel didn't fade away in the sport as many aging athletes did. He went out of the game with his abilities more respected than when he entered in the 1920s. He was named to the NHL's Second All-Star team. He was second in voting for the Hart Trophy as league MVP.

He did not slow down in retirement either. His family grew to five children — Constance, Diane, Lionel Jr., David, and Brian. He bought into an investment firm in Toronto. He even went west with his brother to invest in an oil field. After a childhood spent in poverty, he didn't have to worry about money ever again.

During his sporting years, Lionel had met many important people. Some helped him in business. But it was becoming friends with Mitchell Hepburn that took his life in a new direction. Hepburn was the leader of the Liberal Party in Ontario vying for the job of premier in the 1937 election.

Honouring Lionel Conacher

Lionel has been elected to the Canadian Sports Hall of Fame, Hockey Hall of Fame, Canadian Football Hall of Fame, and Canadian Lacrosse Hall of Fame. Every year the members of the Canadian Press vote to decide a Canadian male athlete of the year. The winner is awarded the Lionel Conacher Award.

Hepburn talked Lionel into running in the election. Lionel got the Liberal nomination for the Toronto-Bracondale riding, the same poor neighbourhood he had once lived in.

Lionel won the election by a slim 37 votes. While in office he made sure he helped the poor families in his riding.

In 1945, Lionel ran in the federal election in the Toronto-Trinity riding. He lost, but that did not stop him. He ran again in 1949 and won. He was re-elected in 1953.

In 1950 Canadian Press staff writer Jack Sullivan organized a national poll to select the outstanding athletes of the first half-century. He asked 43 sportswriters and sportscasters across Canada to name the greatest athletes, greatest teams, and greatest events from 1900 to 1950. They would also decide who was the greatest female athlete and greatest male athlete of

A Toronto-area billboard asking people to vote for Lionel in the upcoming election.

the half-century.

Newspapers across Canada carried the results as they were released.

Fanny "Bobbie" Rosenfeld, an Olympic track and field star, was voted the greatest female athlete of the half-century.

For greatest male athlete of the half-century, Lionel won by a huge majority. He received 33 votes. In second place was Olympic runner Percy Williams with only two votes. The vote confirmed what had been known for a long time. Lionel had no equal.

Lionel Conacher was also voted the half-century greatest football player and received votes as greatest lacrosse player.

"Time was the only thing that placed any limit on his talent and even then he could cram more into a day than any ordinary man," wrote the *Star*. "If you listed Conacher's feats and sent the story to Hollywood they'd turn them down as too fantastic."

Lionel's achievements in life were greater than any Frank Merriwell story. The whole series of Merriwell stories could not compare to what Lionel had done over his lifetime. Football, hockey,

baseball, lacrosse, and boxing championships were followed by successful
businesses and a career in politics.

In the year 2000 there was a vote for the
greatest athlete of the 20th century. By this

Lionel as MP for Toronto-Trinity.

time, Lionel's great moments in sport were largely forgotten. Unlike sport stars of today, there were no visual recordings of Lionel's feats.

Wayne Gretzky was named greatest male athlete of the century. Lionel finished fourth in voting. He was the only true multi-sport athlete in the top ten.

Milt Dunnell, former sports editor of the *Toronto Star*, said, "These days, with all the seasons overlapping, the amount of money involved and the need to specialize, nobody will even get a chance to do what Conacher did."

Epilogue

Lionel would always be known as the boy who left Jesse Ketchum Park. But, the Park never left him. It was considered a poor neighbourhood. But to Lionel it was rich in so many other ways. Most important was the fact that it was the neighbourhood where Lionel first discovered sport.

His father and mother had to work hard for the family to survive. It showed Lionel that hard work was the way to get ahead in life. For his parents it ensured the family had a roof over their heads and food on their table. For Lionel, hard work and dedication to sport made him Toronto's top athlete by the time he turned twenty.

As an adult, Lionel became one of Canada's greatest all-round athletes. He won championships in football, hockey, and baseball. Whenever he suited up for a team people knew he would be the star performer. His hard work as an athlete eventually put a roof over his own family's head and food on their table.

An athlete during this time period might have played two or three sports at a high level over their career. Lionel played five different sports professionally. This included the introduction of professional football to Canada.

By the time he retired he was considered more than just a great athlete. People respected him. This helped him go into a new career as a politician. With this job he returned to his old neighbourhood to help out the people that needed it.

But sport would always be a part of his life. It wasn't something he could just forget. He would never turn down a chance to play lacrosse or hockey with friends. He would organize old-timers games to help raise money for various charities. At these events he would be a little older and slower, but he always kept up the determination to win.

Lionel brought together his political and sporting sides on May 26, 1954. On that day a crowd gathered on the lawn of Parliament Hill in Ottawa. It wasn't for an important speech or protest. They wanted to watch the annual House of Commons vs. Press Gallery baseball game. The team of Members of Parliament (MPs) played journalists to raise money for the pageboys in parliament.

Some might have been there to watch

Lionel play one more time. As an MP, he wanted to play in the benefit. But before the game, Lionel almost dropped out. Quitting was something he never did.

"I don't feel so good and I really should go home," said Lionel, who had just turned 54. "I promised the fellows I'd play in the game."

Lionel complained of a slight pain in his chest. It still hurt before he came to bat in the top of the sixth inning.

"C'mon, Lionel, we're not getting as many homers as we used to," called out a fellow MP.

"I guess we're getting older," Lionel replied.

He swung hard at two pitches and missed.

He scowled.

"Smile a little," yelled another player.

But Lionel did not smile. He was playing as though the game was as important as the World Series.

He lifted the next pitch high into left field. The crowd cheered him and laughed at the left fielder that bobbled the ball. Lionel went into third base standing up.

"He looked pretty grey when he came into third," said the third baseman. "I said to him, 'That was a great clout.' He didn't answer. A second or two later he fell."

Some thought Lionel was pulling a stunt. But any laughter quickly stopped. The lawn of Parliament Hill was suddenly stilled.

Lionel Conacher died 20 minutes later on the way to Ottawa General Hospital. It was the end of the fabulous career of the Big Train.

Shock struck everyone who heard the news. Tributes poured in from across North America.

"A symbol is gone," wrote the *Globe*. "Canada's symbol of prowess and versatility in sport."

Lionel's brother Charlie said, "He would tackle anything from facing Jack Dempsey in the boxing ring, to taking on Tim Buck in a political ring, to battling half the world-champion New York Rangers hockey team in Madison Square Garden and he'd give it everything he had."

Lionel's memorial service was held at St. John's Anglican Church. The church was built to hold 700 people. It didn't take long for the building to fill and overflow.

There were many honoured greats on hand, including politicians and sports figures. There were also ordinary people who had known Lionel as a sports figure, a friend, and a neighbour. And Lionel's parents and family were there. "To them Lionel was above all a fine son and an excellent father," wrote Red Burnett of the *Toronto Star.*

This became a time to remember him as a great athlete. Whole pages in newspapers were devoted to the retelling of his sporting career. This brought back people's memories of what it was like to watch the Big Train dash down the football field. And the people who never had the chance to witness his greatness would wish they had.

It was said there would never be another all-round athlete like Lionel Conacher again. It was easy to agree. He was one of a kind.

Glossary

Assist: In hockey, a pass that leads to a teammate scoring a goal.

Ball carrier: In football, any player who is carrying the ball.

Blocking: In hockey, when a player gets in the way of another player using his body.

Boer War: A war fought in the country of South Africa from 1889–1902.

Breakaway: In hockey, when a player has the puck and there are no defenders other than the goalie between him and the goal.

Championship: A competition, or contest, for a title or prize.

Check/checking: In hockey, any contact to get the puck away from, or to slow down, an opponent.

Defencemen: In hockey, two players who help the goalie guard against attack.

End zone: In football, the areas at each end of the field between the goal line and the end of the field of play.

Exhibition game: A game that is not part of the regular season.

Expansion: In hockey, the addition of teams to the NHL.

Field goal: In football, when the ball is kicked through the uprights in the opponent's end zone.

Fighting: In hockey, a penalty when two or more players drop their sticks and gloves to fight.

Forward pass: In football, a pass in the direction of the opponent's end zone.

Fumble: In football, when a player drops the ball.

Gangrene: An infection that causes the decay of an area on the human body.

Goal line: In football, the line that must be crossed with the ball in order to score a touchdown.

Heart attack: When the blood supply to part of the heart is stopped. This is the main cause of death in both men and women.

Intermediate league: The middle level of play between junior league and senior league.

Jugular vein: A vein in the neck that takes blood from the head back to the heart.

Lateral pass: In football, a sideways or rearwards throwing of the ball.

League: A collection of sports teams that compete against one another.

Line of scrimmage: In football, an imaginary line that each team cannot cross until the play begins. It is on this line that each teams lines up to start the play.

MVP: A player voted as Most Valuable Player.

Opponent: The challenging, or rival, player or team.

Overtime: In hockey, an additional period of play used to break a tie.

Penalty: In hockey, the punishment of a player for breaking rules by removing the player from the game for a period of time.

Reception: In football, when a player catches the ball.

Slashing: In hockey and lacrosse, striking an opponent's arms or lower body with the stick.

Spectator: A person viewing a game.

Tackle: In football, the act of forcing the ball carrier to the ground.

Touchdown: In football, the main way a team scores points. To score a touchdown, one team must take the football into their opponent's end zone.

Yard: In football, a measure of distance on the field.

Acknowledgements

Technology has really made research a lot more accessible, especially when you live in the wilderness of Northwestern Ontario.

The primary research was done through various online newspaper archives. This included the *Toronto Star*, *Globe and Mail*, *New York Times*, and *Chicago Tribune*. *Macleans* magazine was also a valuable source of information.

I knew I was on the right track with my research when I read Dan Morrow's article on Lionel Conacher in the *Journal of Sports History* and Frank Cosentino's 1981 biography about Lionel Conacher. I had come up with most of the same information as these researchers while reading through over a thousand newspaper articles involving Lionel. But, I did find certain tidbits of information in their research that helped with this book.

I would like to thank my wife Shelley for her complete understanding when it comes to my writing career. Her positive attitude has pulled me through some difficult deadlines.

I would also like to thank children's editor Faye Smailes. It has been fun. I am sad to see you go, but you're on to bigger and better things.

About the Author

Richard Brignall is a journalist from Kenora, Ontario, who has written for such publications as *Cottage Life* and *Outdoor Canada*. He was previously the sports reporter for the *Kenora Daily Miner and News*. He is the author of the Recordbooks volume *Forever Champions*, and co-author, with John Danakas, of the Recordbooks volume *Small Town Glory*.

Photo Credits

We gratefully acknowledge the following sources for permission to reproduce the images in this book.

Canadian Football Hall of Fame: p 31, p 63, p 116, back cover (middle)
City of Toronto Archives: p 74 and back cover (bottom): Series 1057, Item 2871; p 96: Fonds 1266, Item 25983; p 142: Fonds 1244, Item 8200
Library and Archives Canada: p 23, p 56, p 92, p 144
Richard Brignall: p 100, p 124, front cover (top)

Index